OTIS & SYDNEY
AND THE BEST BIRTHDAY EVER

By Laura Numeroff

Illustrated by Dan Andreasen

Abrams Books for Young Readers
New York

The illustrations in this book were made
with pen and ink with digital coloring.

Library of Congress Cataloging-in-Publication Data

Numeroff, Laura Joffe.
Otis & Sydney and the best birthday ever /
by Laura Numeroff ; illustrated by Dan Andreasen.
p. cm.
Summary: Otis plans a surprise party for his best friend, Sydney,
and although he has put the wrong date on the invitations and no one else comes,
the two still have a wonderful time together.
ISBN 978-0-8109-8959-7
[1. Best friends—Fiction. 2. Friendship—Fiction.
3. Birthdays—Fiction. 4. Parties—Fiction.
5. Bears—Fiction.] I. Andreasen, Dan, ill. II. Title.
PZ7.N964Bfk 2010
[E]—dc22
2009047199

Text copyright © 2010 Laura Numeroff
Illustrations copyright © 2010
Dan Andreasen

Book design by Chad W. Beckerman

Printed and bound in China
10 9 8 7 6 5 4 3 2 1

Abrams Books for Young Readers are available
at special discounts when purchased in quantity
for premiums and promotions as well as fundraising
or educational use. Special editions can also be created to
specification. For details, contact
specialmarkets@abramsbooks.com
or the address below.

ABRAMS
THE ART OF BOOKS SINCE 1949
115 West 18th Street
New York, NY 10011
www.abramsbooks.com

In memory of my own Otis and Sydney
—L. N.

For Emily
—D. A.

One rainy day, Otis's umbrella broke while he was waiting for the bus.

Sydney invited him to share his.

They soon discovered that they had a lot in common.

They both enjoyed dressing in silly costumes, playing tug-of-war, and jumping on a trampoline.

That's when Otis and Sydney became best friends.

Otis taught Sydney how to play his accordion, and Sydney taught Otis how to play his harmonica.

They loved to make music together.

Every year they gave each other a birthday party.

But this year Otis wanted to do something special. He'd have a surprise party for Sydney!

Otis would invite all their friends over. They would hide, and when Sydney got home, they'd all yell, "Surprise!" Then they would do lots of fun things.

Otis mailed the invitations.

The big day arrived. While Sydney was out, Otis got ready for the party. He decorated the house with balloons, baked a birthday cake, brought costumes down from the attic, and got out the harmonica and accordion.

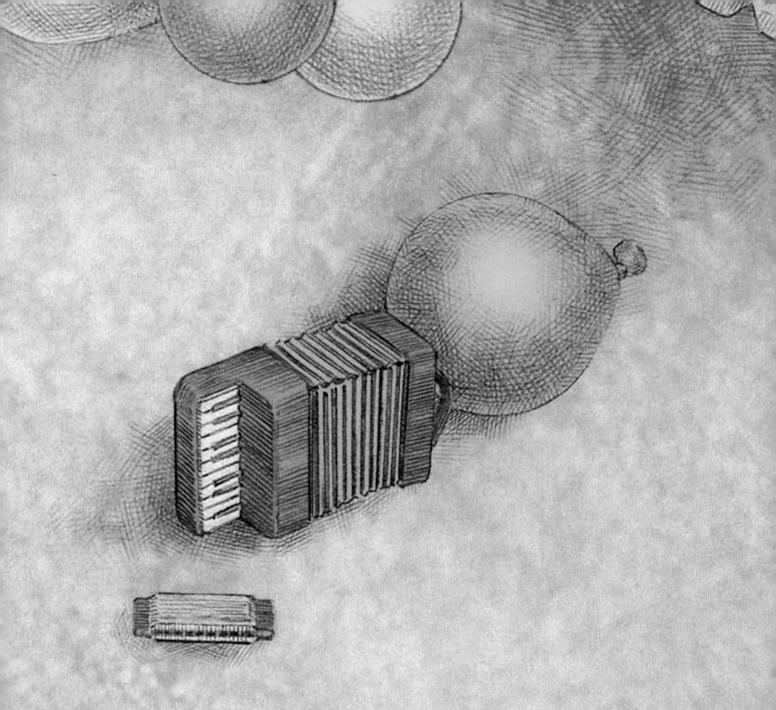

Then he waited for all the guests to arrive.
He waited. And waited. And waited.

"Where is everybody?" he worried.

Suddenly, Otis realized that he
had gotten the date wrong on the
invitations. But it was too late.

Otis heard Sydney coming up the stairs. So he ran behind the couch to hide. Sydney opened the front door and turned on the lights. Then Otis jumped up and yelled, "Surprise!"

"I planned a very special party for you," Otis said.

Sydney smiled. "For me?"

"Yes, a surprise party," said Otis. "I want you to have the best birthday ever."

So they did everything that
Otis had planned for the party.

Otis and Sydney dressed up
in silly costumes, jumped on the
trampoline, and played a game of
tug-of-war.

Then they played the harmonica and accordion.

Soon it was time to open presents. Otis handed
Sydney his gift. Sydney ripped off the wrapping
paper and opened the box. Inside was a bow tie.

Sydney put it on. "Thank you, Otis!" he said.

Then Otis brought out a big chocolate cake.

Sydney blew out the candles. Otis
cut the cake into two pieces.

"Why is there so much cake?" Sydney asked.

"Well . . . I invited all our friends to the party, but no one came," Otis said.

"What happened?" Sydney asked.

"I got the date wrong on the invitations.
I wanted this to be the best birthday ever,"
Otis said sadly, "but instead I ruined it."

"But this *was* the best birthday ever," Sydney said.

"Really?" asked Otis.

"Absolutely," said Sydney. "I got to spend it with you."

Otis smiled.

Sydney smiled, too.

It was the best birthday ever.